SLIP STREAM

SPACE
STATION ALERT

DAVID AND HELEN ORME
Illustrated by ALAN BROWN

EDGE
FRANKLIN WATTS
LONDON·SYDNEY

First published in 2014 by
Franklin Watts
338 Euston Road
London NW1 3BH

Franklin Watts Australia
Level 17/207 Kent Street
Sydney NSW 2000

Text © David and Helen Orme 2014
Illustration © Franklin Watts 2014

A CIP catalogue record for this book is
available from the British Library.

(pb) ISBN: 978 1 4451 3068 2
(library ebook) ISBN: 978 1 4451 3069 9

Series Editors: Adrian Cole and Jackie Hamley
Series Advisors: Diana Bentley and Dee Reid
Series Designer: Peter Scoulding

1 3 5 7 9 10 8 6 4 2

Printed in China

Franklin Watts is a division of
Hachette Children's Books,
an Hachette UK company.
www.hachette.co.uk

CONTENTS

CHAPTER 1

SPACE STATION DUTY

Chris and Rob were on space station duty.

It was a lonely job. It could be boring too.

"Just working and eating and sleeping," said Chris.

"At least we have got the Internet to keep in touch," said Rob.

Chris and Rob used the Internet most of the day. They used it for work and to talk to their mates back on Earth.

And, of course, they used it for games.

CHAPTER 2
DIRECT HIT!

Chris and Rob got a great view of the Earth from the space station.

"Look at that!" said Rob. "A hurricane — a big one. It's heading for ground control. I had better let them know!"

Rob radioed Earth. "A hurricane — coming your way!" he said.

"Thanks Rob," said Ground Control. "We know about the hurricane. Everything is ready down here."

Then came the crash.

"What on Earth was that?" shouted Rob.

"It wasn't on Earth — it was up here!" yelled

Chris. "We have been hit. Hold on!"

CHAPTER 3
SYSTEM FAIL

"Let's check the damage," said Chris.

They opened a storeroom door and looked around. A metal pipe was bent in. They could hear a hissing noise.

"We are losing air! Check life support!" Rob cried.

"We have 12 hours of air left. Get onto Ground Control, quick. We need to get out of here!" shouted Rob.

Ground Control had a problem.

"It's the hurricane. Sorry guys, but there's no way we can launch a rocket. Can you fix the damage?"

Chris and Rob tried, but it was impossible.

It was getting harder and harder to breathe.

They soon began to feel dizzy. There was
no way they could survive.

CHAPTER 4

BACK FROM THE DEAD

Chris woke up. He was lying on the floor.

He had a headache, but he was OK.

He could breathe!

Rob was lying next to him. He opened his eyes.

"We are alive! How come?" said Rob.

They checked the damaged pipe.

It was fixed!

Rob sat at the computer to send a message

to Ground Control. There was a message on

his screen.

"Hi there guys. Sorry we hit your space station.

Too busy looking down at your great planet!

Hope we fixed the pipe OK.

P.S. Not all aliens are unfriendly!

P.P.S Your Internet is brilliant, isn't it! ☺ "

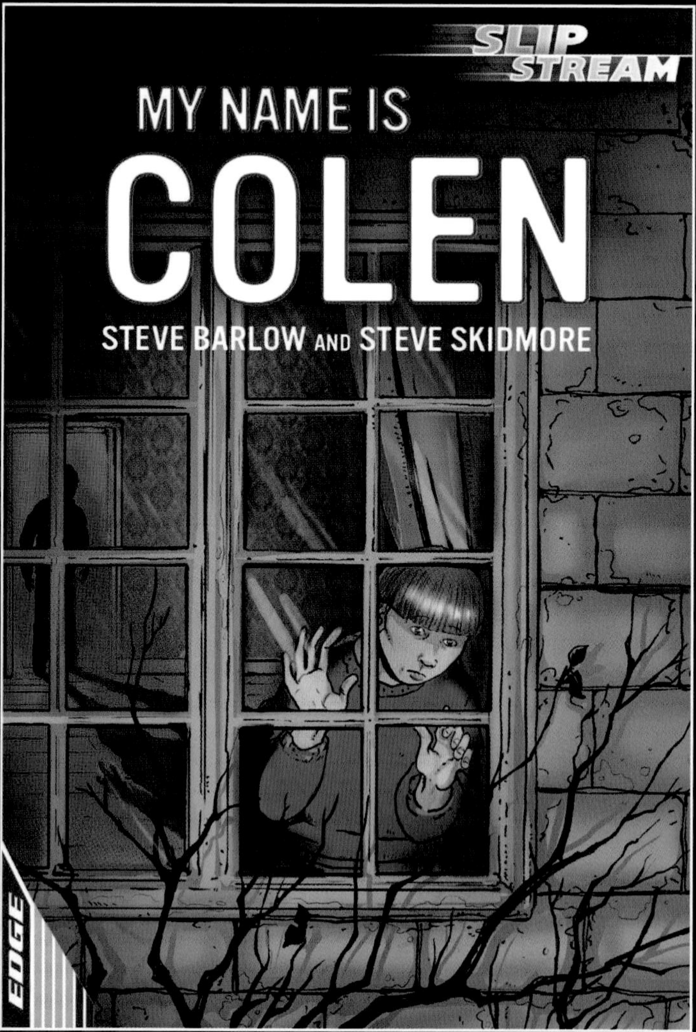
SLIP STREAM
MY NAME IS
COLEN
STEVE BARLOW AND STEVE SKIDMORE
EDGE

n is not your usual kid next door. When Becca tries to make friends, she knows that things are definitely not right.

Why does he never go out? Why is his uncle so strict? And why do Colen and his uncle look so similar?

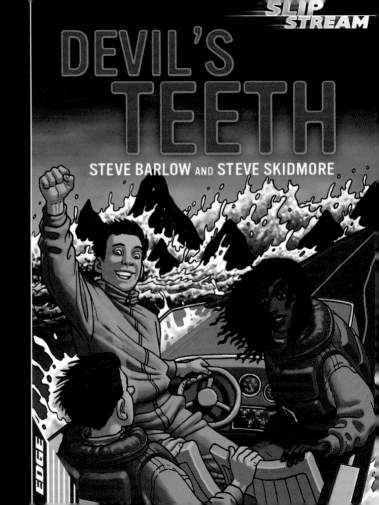

When Owen agrees to go for a trip with Emma on Jeb's boat, he has no idea how reckless Jeb will be. Now a storm is coming and they are dangerously close to the Devil's Teeth rocks. How can Owen get them back to shore alive?

EDGE
FRANKLIN WATTS

LONDON·SYDNEY

About SLIP STREAM

Slipstream is a series of expertly levelled books designed for pupils who are struggling with reading. Its unique three-strand approach through fiction, graphic fiction and non-fiction gives pupils a rich reading experience that will accelerate their progress and close the reading gap.

At the heart of every Slipstream fiction book is a great story. Easily accessible words and phrases ensure that pupils both decode and comprehend, and the high interest stories really engage older struggling readers.

Whether you're using Slipstream Level 2 for Guided Reading or as an independent read, here are some suggestions:

1. Make each reading session successful. Talk about the text before the pupil starts reading. Introduce any unfamiliar vocabulary.

2. Encourage the pupil to talk about the book using a range of open questions. For example, what is the most exciting job they can think of? What is the most boring?

3. Discuss the differences between reading fiction, graphic fiction and non-fiction. Which do they prefer?

For guidance, SLIPSTREAM Level 2 –Space Station Alert has been approximately measured to:

National Curriculum Level: 2b
Reading Age: 7.6–8.0
Book Band: Purple

ATOS: 2.3*
Guided Reading Level: I
Lexile® Measure (confirmed): 300L

*Please check actual Accelerated Reader™ book level and quiz availability at www.arbookfind.co.uk